AF783378

नन्हें कलमकार

(एक आशावादी विध्यार्थी सूर्यान्श को समर्पित)

ऋतु थपलियाल 'सुदेवस्तु'

PG PUBLICATION

दिल्ली-110089, (भारत)

संस्करण : 2020
ISBN : 9789389984194

प्रखर गूँज पब्लिकेशन
एच-3/2, सेक्टर-18, रोहिणी, दिल्ली-110089
दूरभाष : **7982710571, 7838505899, 011-27851059**

प्रथम संस्करण : 2020

© सम्बंधित रचनाकार के अधीन

आवरण : दुर्गाप्रसाद

नन्हें कलमकार

***By* : Ritu Thapliyal 'Sudevastu'**

Published by
PRAKHAR GOONJ PUBLICATION
Delhi-110089
E-mail : prakhargoonj@gmail.com
sinha.neelu123@gmail.com
Ph. : 011-27851059, 7982710571, 7838505899

इस पुस्तक के किसी भी हिस्से को प्रकाशक अथवा लेखक की पूर्व अनुमति के बिना इलेक्ट्रॉनिक अथवा किसी अन्य माध्यम द्वारा पुनः प्राप्ति समेत किसी भी रूप में प्रतिलिपिकृत, अनुवादित अथवा संगृहीत नहीं किया जा सकता है और न ही किसी भी रूप में अथवा किसी भी माध्यम से इसे प्रसारित किया जा सकता है। ऐसा किए जाने पर सम्बंधित के विरुद्ध कानूनी कार्यवाही की जा सकती है।

क्रम तालिका

शुभारंभ

मेरे अपने अध्यापन काल में एक भाव हमेशा सर्वोपरि रहा है की विध्यार्थियों की चमत्कारी व ऊर्जावान दुनिया से कुछ सीखना है और अपने अनुभव की दुनिया से उन्हें परिचित करवाना है। आज भी जब घर से निकलती हूँ तो समय योजना और पाठ योजना देखना कभी नहीं भूलती हूँ। जब विध्यालय पहुँचती हूँ तो इन नन्हें नवांकुरों को देखकर मन मोर की भाँति पंख फैलाने को आतुर रहता है। ऐसा लगता मानो अपने पंखों के भीतर इन्हें छिपाकर इनकी सकारात्मक ऊर्जा का अनुभव कर लूँ। नन्हें-नन्हें नवांकुरों की आभा देखकर लगता है अपना सारा ज्ञान इनकी जड़ों में डाल दूँ ताकि यह स्वस्थ भविष्य का फल निर्मित कर सके। शिक्षणकाल के दौरान यह विचार एक जुनून की तरह मेरे व्यक्तित्व पर भी हावी हो गया है की मुझे इन नन्ही पंखुरियों को जोड़कर उनकी सुगंध में बह जाना है। उनके कंटको को खुद ही उनसे अलग कर देना है।

पठन-पाठन के इस दौर में मैं हमेशा यह सोचती हूँ की कैसे यह नन्हें- नन्हें हाथ स्वयं से लिख सकेंगे? कैसे यह इन अक्षरों की दुनिया में तालमेल बनाएँगे। कैसे यह सोच की लहरों को पार करेंगे? कैसे यह जीवन की पगडंडी पर चलना सीखेंगे। यह एक ऐसी चिंता है जिसके लिए मुझे धैर्य का दामन पकड़े रहना होता है। मात्र अक्षर ज्ञान देना ही शिक्षा नहीं है, बल्कि व्यक्तित्व के विकास के साथ-साथ विध्यार्थी की सकारात्मक सोच का विकास होना भी आवशयक है। हमारे निदेशक महोदय डॉक्टर 'सुबोध थपलियाल' स्वयं पारंपरिक कक्षाओं में दी जाने वाली शिक्षा के अतिरिक्त बाह्य वातावरण के माध्यम से दी जाने वाली शिक्षा पर ज़ोर देते है, इसलिए विध्यार्थियों के समुचित विकास को ध्यान में रखते हुए विध्यालय में मेरे मार्गदर्शन में ही अनेक प्रकार की गतिविधियां होती रही है। इन सब के बीच मुझे यही ख्याल बार-बार आता की यह गतिविधियां कुछ ही बच्चों के व्यक्तित्व का विकास करने में सहायक हो रही है, बाकी विध्यार्थियों को प्रेरणा

देने के लिए और क्या संभव प्रयासकिए जा सकते है। विध्यार्थी गतिविधियों का हिस्सा तो बनते थे, पर कुछ ही समय पश्चात वह स्वयं के ही कार्यों को भूल जाते थे। जो विध्यार्थी गतिविधियों में भाग नहीं ले रहे थे उनके सामने समस्या यह थी की वह पठन और लेखन दोनों में ही आत्मविश्वास का परिचय नहीं दे रहे थे। विध्यार्थियों को किस प्रकार पठन और लेखन से जोड़ा जाए यह समस्या भी मेरे सामने थी और मुझे इसका समाधान ढूँढना था।

इसी दौरान विध्यालय की वार्षिक परीक्षा भी नजदीक आ गई थी। मैंने विचार किया की यदि विध्यार्थियों में वैचारिक क्षमता का विकास करना है तो उन्हें सबसे पहले "सोचना" सीखना होगा ताकि अपने आस-पास के वातावरण को समझकर वह लिख सके। हिन्दी व अंग्रेजी भाषा में रचनात्मक खंड होते है। मैंने इसी खंड से प्रारम्भ किया। यह विचार एक पंथ और दो काज साबित हुआ। इससे विध्यार्थियों की परीक्षा की तैयारी के साथ-साथ उनमे लेखन के प्रति रुचि और आस-पास के वातावरण को ध्यान में रखकर सोचने की क्षमता भी जाग्रत की जा सकी। मेरे निर्देशन में रचनात्मक खंड की कार्यशाला प्रारम्भ की गई। यह कार्यशाला पंद्रह दिन तक चली। इस कार्यशाला के दौरान विध्यार्थियों को लेखन से संबंधित सही प्रारूप सिखाए गए और उनसे गतिविधियां भी करवाई गई। कार्यशाला के दौरान अंग्रेजी विषय की एक अध्यापिका श्रीमती हर्षल ने अंग्रेजी विषय में कहानी लिखने के लिए कक्षा तीन से चार के विध्यार्थियों को कहा था। पहले-पहल विध्यार्थी पुस्तकालय जाकर पुस्तक समीक्षा लिखने लगे। जब उन्होने मुझे यह गतिविधि दिखाई तो मैंने उन्हे सुझाव दिया की यदि विध्यार्थी अपने आस-पास के वातावरण में हो रही घटनाओं का अनुभव कर लिखने का प्रयास करेगा तो वह सहजता से लिख सकेगा। मुझे एक विचार और आया की क्यो न इन नन्हें लेखकों को प्रोत्साहित किया जाए और इन नन्हें कलमकारों को एक साथ जोड़ दिया जाए, इसलिए मैंने निर्णय लिया की इन सभी के लेखन को एक किताब में सहेज कर अनमोल धरोहर का रूप दे दिया जाएगा। तब मेरे

द्वारा सभी को निर्देश दिया गया की दूसरी किताबों की कहानियाँ नहीं बल्कि खुद के जीवन से जुड़ी कहानियाँ लिखी जाये। परिणाम बहुत ही सुखद रहा। श्रीमती हर्षल ने विध्यार्थियों द्वारा लिखी गई कहानियाँ और कविताएं मुझे दिखाई। उनकी यह रचनाएँ देखकर मेरा मन भावविभोर हो गया।

अथक प्रयास के बाद मैं नन्हें कलमकारों को एक सुनहरा पृष्ठ देने में कामयाब हो सकी हूँ। प्रथम प्रयास में हमने कुछ ही कहानियाँ व कविताएं ली है। यदि मेरा यह प्रयास विध्यार्थियों में लिखने व पढ़ने की प्रेरणा साबित हो जाता है तो मैं अपने आपको धन्य समझूंगी और इस दिशा में अपना अगला कदम जल्दी ही उठाने का प्रयास करूंगी।

मैं इन नन्हें कलमकारों को हार्दिक बधाई देती हूँ और इनके सफल भविष्य की कामना करती हूँ। इन सभी के अभिभावकों का भी मैं धन्यवाद देती हूँ जिन्होंने हमारे इस प्रयास को सफल बनाने में सहयोग दिया।

आशा है की यह पुस्तक नन्हें विध्यार्थियों के जीवन में प्रेरणा की किरणें बनकर उनके जीवन को प्रकाशित कर सकने में सहायक होगी।

ऋतु थपलियाल 'सुदेवस्तु'

FOREWORD

"There are many little ways to enlarge your child's world. Love of books is the best of all." – Jacqueline Kennedy

Behind every story, there is an inspiration. The story is the pen-picture of the experiences of the writer.The experiences are conveyed in the form of words. The story not only enhances creativity but also showcases his imagination when the writer is a 9-10 years old. It also helps the children hone their language skills. This is my long term thought process where I wanted my students to write stories in the form of a book. I also wanted these storybooks to be displayed in the Annual Exhibition. I shared my thought with respected Ms.RituThapliyal, Head of the Primary Department, Delhi Public School, Gandhidham. The idea was welcomed with cheer. Encouragingly enough, she has takenan initiative to motivate languages as she has already had idea but in a different way. She advised me to ask the students to write their own imaginative storieswith the belief that their confidence, phonics, grammar and reading skills will get highlighted. She also added that kids should be able to write what they want to write and giving kids a motivation to write is rather essential. The explanation and guidelines of the activity were already given to the students in the class. I encouraged and guidedthe students to write both stories and poems. I received 20 stories and 3 poems from the students. An anthology of top stories and poems have been put together in this book.

My heart-felt thanks to dear Ritu Madam, Head of the Primary Department, Delhi Public School, Gandhidhamfor taking this project to another level. I would fail in my duty if I do not extend my hearty thanks to honourable Dr. SubodhThapliyal, Director, Delhi Public School, Gandhidham, forinspiring me through his tremendous initiative DEAR 'Drop Everything And Read' to come up with this thought. It is needless to mention that the campaign 'Vache Gujarat' by then Chief Minister and current Prime Minister ShriNarendraModiji, also played a good amount of inspiration.

I also express my sincere gratitude to all the students, parents and well-wishers for their unstinted support without which this would not have been possible. It is indeed a proud moment for me to be part of this initiative.

Regards

Harshal Thaker

English Teacher

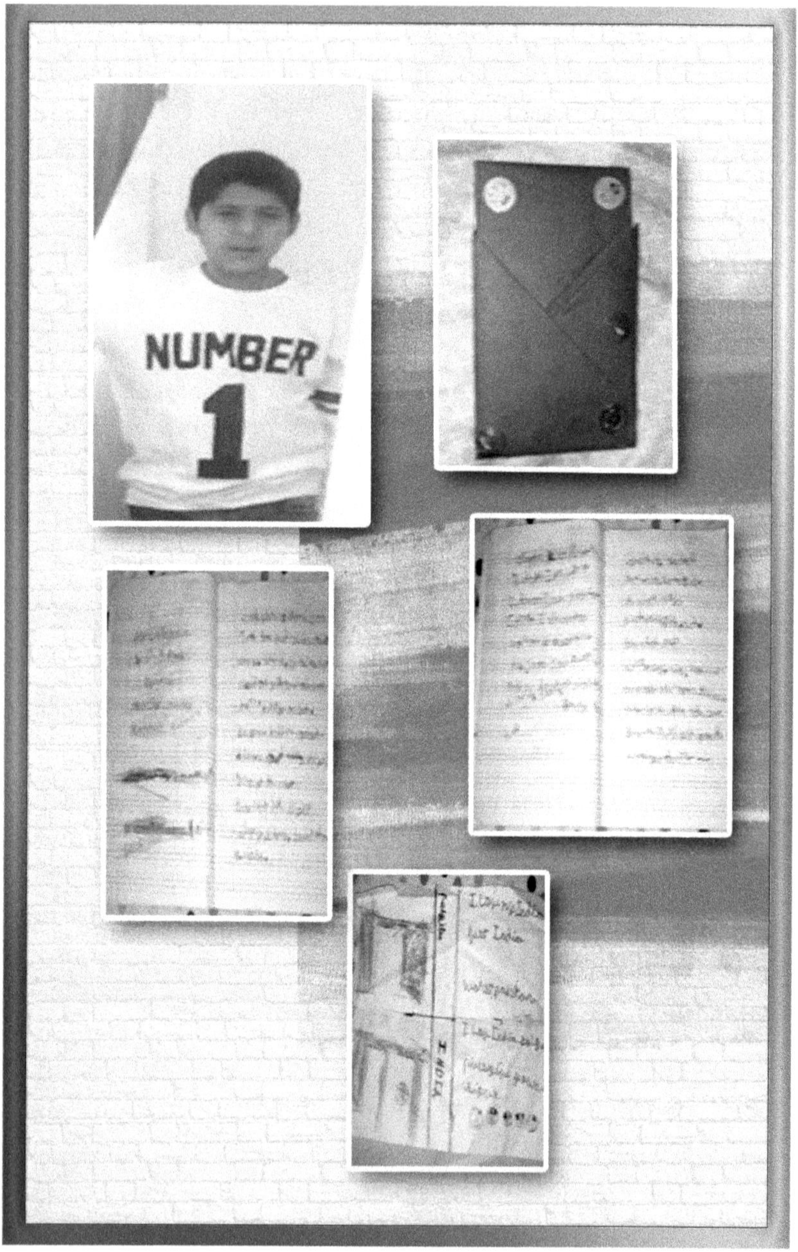
NUMBER
1

मेरी प्रेरणा - सूर्यान्श

जीवन की आपाधापी में आप कभी हताश और निराश हो जाते है और यह बात कब आपका स्वभाव बन जाती है आपको पता ही नहीं चलता है। हम भूल जाते है की हर समस्या का समाधान होता है। बस अपनी दृढ़ इच्छाशक्ति को धैर्य के जल से सींचना होता है।

अपने शिक्षण काल के दौरान कई ऐसी घटनाएँ घटी है जिनसे मुझे प्रेरणा मिली है या मैं यह भी कह सकती हूँ की इन प्रेरणाओं ने मुझे विपरीत परिस्थितियों से लड़ना सिखाया है। यदि आप अध्यापक है तो सुबह-सुबह आप अनेक देवपुंजों से मिलते है और जीवन के सत्य-असत्य की परिभाषा को समझने का प्रयास करते है।

ऐसे ही एक देवपुंज से मेरी मुलाक़ात हुई है। मैंने स्वयंसेवी कार्यकर्ता के रूप में प्राथमिक अध्यक्षा का कार्य भार दिल्ली पब्लिक स्कूल, गांधी धाम में संभाला ही था की एक दिन कक्षा चार की अध्यापिका ने बताया की उनकी कक्षा में एक विध्यार्थी है जिसको ज्यादा समय देना होता है और परीक्षा के समय पर तो ज्यादा ही ध्यान देना होता है, परंतु परीक्षा के समय क्योंकि अध्यापिका को सभी विध्यार्थियों पर ध्यान देना होता है, इसलिए इस विध्यार्थी को परीक्षा में पूर्णरूप से प्रश्नपत्र पढ़कर सहायता करना संभव नहीं हो पाता है। मैंने यह सुनकर तुरंत एक अतिरिक्त अध्यापिका का प्रबंध करवा दिया, जो विध्यार्थी के साथ अलग से बैठकर उसकी सहायता करने वाली थी। इस घटना के बाद मैं अपने कार्य में व्यस्त हो गई। हालांकि मैं इस विध्यार्थी की कक्षा में प्रतिदिन जाती थी, परंतु मुझे सभी कुछ सामान्य लगता था। उसकी मुस्कुराहट में एक कशिश थी, जो मुझे सुखद अनुभव करवाती थी।

परीक्षा का दिन भी आ गया और निर्धारित की गई योजना के अनुसार विध्यार्थी को सहायक अध्यापिका दे दी गई थी। इस प्रबंध का परिणाम सुखद रहा। परीक्षा परिणाम के दिन विध्यार्थी की कक्षा अध्यापिका

के चेहरे पर एक अनोखी चमक थी। वह विध्यार्थी के अंक देखकर बहुत खुश थी। अध्यापिका मेरे पास यह सुखद संदेश लेकर आई, तब वह बार-बार मेरा धन्यवाद कर रही थी की मैंने ऐसा करके विध्यार्थी को ही नहीं बल्कि उसके अभिभावक को भी खुशी प्रदान की है। मुझे ऐसा लगा जैसे मैंने बहुत ही कठिन परीक्षा को पार कर दिया है। पहली बार लगा की मैं एक विध्यार्थी की प्रगति में सहायक बन सकने में कामयाब रही हूँ।

विध्यार्थी अगली कक्षा में पहुँच गया था। अगले सत्र में भी सी. बी. एस. सी. बोर्ड के अनुसार विध्यालय में समयांतराल में परीक्षाएँ होने लगी। इस विशेष विध्यार्थी को प्रत्येक परीक्षा में एक सहायक अध्यापिका दी जाती रही। कक्षा का स्तर ऊँचा होने के कारण एक परीक्षा के दौरान इस विध्यार्थी का प्रश्नपत्र पूरा नहीं हो पाया था। समय समाप्त हो चुका था और सभी से प्रश्नपत्र ले लिए गए थे। सभी विध्यार्थी अपनी-अपनी बसों में घर जाने के लिए बैठ गए थे। मैं अपनी प्रतिदिन के कार्यानुसार परीक्षा के अंत मे उस कक्ष में गई जहाँ पर यह विध्यार्थी बैठकर परीक्षा दे रहा था। सहायक अध्यापिका ने बताया विध्यार्थी का कार्य पूरा नहीं हुआ है और समय भी समाप्त हो गया है, परंतु विध्यार्थी पूरा प्रश्नपत्र हल करना चाहता है। मैं एक क्षण को रुक गई मुझे लगा की जहाँ सारे विध्यार्थी घर जाने को आतुर हुये बैठे है, इनमे से कुछ लापरवाह भी होंगे जिन्हें परीक्षा का महत्व भी नहीं ज्ञात होगा, वही यह धैर्य के साथ बैठा है। इसे इस समय मात्र यह दिखाई दे रहा की इसे अपना प्रश्नपत्र हल करना है।

मैं उसके पास गई और उससे पूछा -"तुम सचमुच में ऐसा करना चाहते हो, तुम्हें घर नहीं जाना है।"

उसने "नहीं" में अपना सिर हिला दिया और कहा -"मैम मैं लिखना चाहता हूँ।"

मैं स्तब्ध थी और कहीं न कहीं मन में खुश हो रही थी, इसलिए नहीं की वो लिखना चाहता है, बल्कि इसलिए की वो हार नहीं मानना चाहता है। वो परीक्षा देना चाहता है। आज जहाँ सामान्य विध्यार्थी अपने मार्ग से भटके

हुए है। जिन्हें प्रतिदिन पढ़ाई का महत्व समझाना होता है, वही यह देवपुंज डटकर बैठा है और हर हालत में अपनी परीक्षा देना चाहता है।

मैंने उससे कहा- 'ठीक है ..... मैं आपकी मम्मी को फोन कर देती हूँ, वो आपको लेने आ जाएंगी।"

ऐसा सुनते ही उसके चेहरे पर एक चमक आ गई, जैसे वो निश्चिंत हो गया था और वो अपना प्रश्नपत्र लिखने लगा। मैंने उसकी कक्षा अध्यापिका को निर्देश दिया की विध्यार्थी को समय दिया जाएगा, तब तक विध्यार्थी के माता-पिता को सूचित कर दिया जाए।

इस घटना के बाद से मेरी जिज्ञासा उस आशावादी विध्यार्थी के लिए बढ़ गई। अब मैं प्रतिदिन उसकी कक्षा में भिक्षुक बनकर जाने लगी हूँ और वो जो भी दक्षिणा में मुझे देता है मैं उसको अपनी झोली में समेटकर ले आती हूँ। हर बार वो मुझे अपनी नई खोज या कार्य से परिचित करवाता है और मैं आश्चर्य से घिर जाती हूँ। कभी वो मुझे अपनी ड्रायिंग दिखाता है, कभी अपनी लिखी कहानी। कभी बताता है की उसने यू-ट्यूब से कैमरा बनाना सीखा है फिर अपने हाथों से बना कैमरा मुझे दिखाता है। जब मैं कहती हूँ की मुझे भी बनाना सिखाओ, तो मासूमियत से कहता है मैं आपको 'सिक्स्थ क्लास में सिखाऊँगा।' मैं उसके आत्मविश्वास को देखकर हैरान हो जाती हूँ।

हरबार मैं उसके माता-पिता के आगे नतमस्तक हो जाती हूँ। जहां आज हम सबकुछ होते हुये भी निराशाओं के घेरे में खड़े है, वही यह आशावादी बच्चा ईश्वर के निर्माण को चुनौती दे रहा है और उसके माता-पिता उसका आत्मबल बनकर उसके साथ खड़े है।

"सूर्यान्श" वास्तव में सूर्य का ही अंश है। जिस प्रकार सूर्य का तेज सदैव बना रहता है। उसी प्रकार सूर्यान्श की आशा सदैव उसके अस्तित्व की आभा बनी रहती है। मैं इस देवपुंज को हृदय से शुभकामनायें देती हूँ की यह सूर्यकी तरह ही चमकता रहे।

ऋतु थपलियाल 'सुदेवस्तु'

नाम : देवस्य थपलियाल, कक्षा : चार, सत्र : 2019-2020

सब की योग्यता और सच का साथ

एक दिन डायरेक्टर सर हमारी कक्षा में आए। कक्षा में सभी चुपचाप बैठे थे, पर मैं शैतानी कर रहा था।

सर जैसे ही कक्षा में आए मैं अपनी जगह पर बैठ गया।

सर - गुड मॉर्निंग आल ऑफ यू।

बच्चे - गुड मॉर्निंग सर।

सर - अच्छा सब मुझे बताओ की आपकी कक्षा में सबसे ज्यादा चुपचाप रहने वाला और शांत बच्चा कौन है?

बच्चे - सर मनन बंबानी (हम सभी ने एक साथ ज़ोर से कहा) वह ज्यादा

किसी से बात नहीं करता है।

सर - अच्छा अब बताओ सबसे ज्यादा बोलने वाला बच्चा कौन है?

सारी कक्षा चुप थी। कुछ समय बाद मैंने अपना हाथ उठाया।

देवस्य - सर मैं सबसे ज्यादा बोलता हूँ।

सारी कक्षा हँसने लगी ,तब सर ने सबको चुप करवाया।

सर - बहुत खूब देवस्य! सच बोलना सबसे अच्छी बात है और यह साहस का काम भी है। हमे हमेशा सच बोलना चाहिए।

सर ने मेरे सच बोलने पर सारी कक्षा के विध्यार्थियों से मेरे लिए तालियाँ बजवाई।

तभी सर ने कहा -बच्चों सब की खूबी अलग- अलग होती है, इसलिए हमे एक दूसरे से सीखना चाहिए। आज से मनन और देवस्य साथ -साथ बैठेंगे ताकि ये दोनों एक दूसरे की खूबी सीख सके।

शिक्षा- हमे हमेशा सच बोलना चाहिए और सभी से कुछ न कुछ सीखना चाहिए, क्योंकि सभी में अलग- अलग खूबी होती है।

नाम : शॉमली मुखर्जी, कक्षा : पाँच, सत्र : 2019-2020

बदलाव

हमारी वार्षिक परीक्षाएँ चल रही थी, जो साढ़े ग्यारह बजे समाप्त हो जाती थी। मेरी माँ मेरे ही विध्यालय में अध्यापिका है इसलिए परीक्षा समाप्ति के बाद उन्हें दो बजे तक रुककर अपने विधालय के कार्यों को पूरा करना होता था, जिसके कारण मुझे विध्यालय में अपने दोस्तों के साथ खेलने को मिल जाया करता था। एक दिन मैं अपनी परीक्षा होने के बाद विध्यालय के बगीचे में खेलने के लिए गई। मैं वहाँ अपने दोस्तों के साथ खेल रही थी, तभी मेरी नजर बगीचे के कोने में स्थित एक पेड़ पर गई, जहाँ एक छोटी सी लड़की पेड़ की आड़ लेकर खड़ी थी। वह हम सबको खेलते हुये देख रही थी। मैंने उसको अपने पास बुलाया और उससे कहा –'आओ तुम भी हमारे साथ खेलो। 'लेकिन वो डर रही थी और उसने खेलने से मना कर

दिया। तब मैं खुद उसके पास चली गई। मैंने उससे पूछा –'क्या तुम मेरी दोस्त बनोगी। 'उसने "हाँ" में अपना सर हिलाया। फिर मैंने उससे उसका नाम पूछा। उसने बताया की उसका नाम मुस्कान है और वो विध्यालय में काम करने वाले माली अंकल की बेटी है। मुस्कान मेरे दूसरे दोस्तो के साथ भी घुलमिल गई और हम सब खेलने लगे। अगले दिन मेरी दूसरी परीक्षा थी इसलिए मुझे उसकी तैयारी भी करनी थी। मैंने मुसकान से पूछा –'मुस्कान क्या तुम स्कूल जाती हो?' उससे "नहीं" में सिर हिलाया। मुझे बहुत आश्चर्य हुआ। मैंने उससे पूछा की तुम्हें गिनती आती है। उसने नहीं में अपना उत्तर दिया। मुझे फिर बहुत आश्चर्य हुआ की मुस्कान स्कूल नहीं जाती है। मैंने फिर उसकी ओर देखकर कहा –'क्या तुम पढ़ना चाहती हो।' उसने "हाँ" में सर हिलाया। तब मैने उसे अपने साथ पढ़ने बैठा दिया। मुझे बहुत अच्छा लगा की वह बहुत मन लगाकर पढ़ रही थी।

मैंने मन में सोचा की क्यू न मैं इसे रोज पढ़ाया करूँ। फिर तो जब भी मुझे समय मिलता था मैं उसे पढ़ाने बैठ जाया करती थी। ऐसा करके मुझे यह लगा की इस दुनिया में बहुत से बच्चे है जो पढ़ना चाहते है ,पर पढ़ नहीं पा रहे है। लेकिन हम सब जो पढ़ रहे है यदि वह चाहे तो इन बच्चो की मदद कर सकते है। मुस्कान जैसे बच्चों के चेहरे पर खुशी की मुस्कान ला सकते है।

शिक्षा –यदि हम नव पीढी चाहे तो एक दूसरे की मदद करके सभी को साक्षर बना सकते है।।

नाम : अंजलि मिस्त्री, कक्षा : दसवीं, सत्र : 2019-2020

अब सफलता मेरे हाथों में

उस दौर से गुजरी हूँ मैं,
चारों ओर असफलता से घिरी हूँ मैं।
उम्मीद की किरने डूब गई आकाश में,
पहुँच पाऊँगी क्या कभी प्रकाश में।
आ गई देखो! कैसी काल रात्री,
हाय! कैसे सताये मुझे वीभत्स दात्री।

न जाने कब आएगी नई सुबह अब,

शांत हुये अँधियारे में सब के सब।

इस घोर अमावस की रात में,

बैठी हूँ मैं सुनहरे जीवन की आस में।

सिसक- सिसक कर मैं सो गई,

फिर उस रात्री में मैं खो गई।

लड़- झगड़कर अपने आँसुओ से,

नई सुबह हिम्मत जुटाई है अपनी बाजुओ से।

मेरी आँख खुल गई बुलंद आवाजों से,

आ गई नई सुबह, अब सफलता मेरे हाथो में।

Name : Anaisha Aggarwal, Class : III, Year : 2019-2020

THE NAUGHTY SISTERS

Once upon a time there lived two sisters. The elder one was Lily and younger one was Rosy. Both the sisters were very naughty. Theywere fighting now and then. One day in the parent teacher meeting their teacher said that these two sisters are very naughty. Their mother was very upset. She scolded both the girls.

The two sisters got an idea. Both the sisters planned that we will be good girls whenever mother is in the house. The next day they woke up they brushed their teeth quietly and went to school without any noise.The other days they did the same. After few days mother was shocked and thought what's going on. She told her neighbours that the two sisters have been good for few days.

The neighbours didn't trust the mother, but mother asked the neighbours to come home tomorrow. The next day neighbours came to the house and saw that the sisters were fighting but when the mother came inside the house the sisters were behaving nicely.After this mother was upset to see this.

Lateron, the neighbours and the mother understood that when mother is not in the house they fight and when the mother is away they behave like good sisters.

Mother came to know about their plan.But she didn't tell her daughters.Mother made a plan. She pretended that she is going out.She hide herself in the kitchen. The sisters thought mother is not home. The sisters started fighting thinking their mother is not home. They started hitting each other and got hurt badly. Both the girls started crying.

Their mother came and told them that she had been watching them from the kitchen. Both the girls felt bad that they were fighting. They realized their mistake.They apologized to their mother that they will not fight again. After that they became true sisters and lived happily forever.

Moral of the story

We Should Be True with Every one and not Fight with Anyone!!

Name : Anvesha Agarwal, Class : III, Year : 2019-2020

PANCHTANTRA TALES

1. Foolish Sue

Sue was a small stork, who was trained to catch many fishes at a time, but she got fooled very easily.

She always wanted more of everything. One day Sue wanted to shift to another river, but the river she chose was full of crocodiles. She went to the nearest crocodile and asked "who is your leader". The crocodile asked "why?" Sue said I want to live in this river, askmeas many fish as you want. The crocodile said, I am the leader of this river, give me all the fish you have in your lake. Then this river is yours.

Sue rushed to her lake and brought all the fishes. The crocodile quickly ate the fishes and happily crawled away. Sue proudly stood on a rock and shouted, "This is my river now." I asked your leader and he agreed you all have to shift to different lakes and rivers now. A crocodile came forward and said "but this is my river and I am the leader". Sue became very careful from now.

Moral of the story

Strangers can't be trusted.

2. Polly and Paulina

There once lived 2 birds Polly and Paulina. Polly was active but very proud but Paulina was slow and steady.

Proud Polly thought to make Paulina feel very sad.

While Paulina was searching food, Polly thought of painting which Paulina never liked. She challenged her for a painting competition but Paulina was a genius she knew that Polly would do something to make her feel sad. Instead she started preparing herself she did all the work she had when it was finished she would practice painting.

After a week Paulina was ready. It was a huge place to paint. The leader elephant Jumbo was also present in the crowd. All the animals had taken their seats. And the competition began.

Polly and Paulina started. Polly was so fast no one could see what she was doing. But Paulina was so patient and slow when Polly submitted it was not as beautiful as Paulina. Even Jumbo agreed. Polly apologised and improved herself.

Moral of Story

Slow and steady wins the race.

3. Every one can`t be Trusted

Once there was a big black toad. Everyone made fun of him, from the king Lion to the smallest squirrel.

The frog felt offended and said to himself "Oh God, why can't I have a peaceful morning, why do they always trouble me, why can't I trouble them. Every time all animals pass they laugh at me, making me feel sad. All of a sudden he had an idea. This was not to make any one feel sad.It was to make everyone feel sorry. He knew that in which river he lived was very deep. To fool the animals, he said "O my dear animals brothers and sisters today I am not going to annoy you all, but I am going to tell you that in the lake I live can cure my disease and can make you so beautiful that the village people will admire you,

Suddenly a fox came running and widely said "you live in this river, you swim in this river, you drink from this river than why the river didn't cure you, you still have black spots. Now the truth was revealed , all the animals started shouting.

"You lied." "Leave us." The frog apologized and left for ever.

Moral of the Story

Bad deeds are always found by someone.

Name : Diya Agrawal, Class: III, Year : 2019-2020

THE MAGIC SHOW PART I

There was a small school trip for students. Trip was only for classes I to III. All the teachers of class I to III had announced the trip in their respective classes. The amazing part of the trip is 'THE MAGIC SHOW'. The name of magician is KARAN. It's a very natural that students became happy. All the students were very much excited.One day a strange thing happened. Almost all the students were going to see the magic show. Among them only one child was not going with them. The reason was she saw the same magic show last one week ago. So her parents not allowed her to go with classmates. Parents make her understand very kindly. They told the things behind disagreement. The girl became confused. As she knew that her parents were also right. But still she wanted to go with classmates. Finally the day came to see the magic show. As always the girl went to school. She saw that all the students were full of excitement. They were crazy. They brought yummy snacks with them these yum snacks were going to eat while watching the magic show. Soon the class teacher came. The class became silent.' Are you all ready to go to see the magic show? Asked the class teacher. The girl became very sad 'Yes! M'am!' said all the students. Ma'am asked her why she was so upset. She didn't reply. The peon came with the list of students who were coming. The teacher got upset. Among 200 students only one student is not coming. And a student is this girl 'How she will stay, alone in the school'? She'll get bore that is the reason she is upset. These thoughts were coming into mind. M'am took a decision. She took the phone and called the girl's parents.The call was received by her father. M'am asked him why he has not allowed his daughter for the school trip. Father gave the same reason which they have given to his daughter. M'am told the reason behind her call. Among 200 students only their child was not coming. She was very upset. Now the class teacher convinced the father. He agreed for the school trip. The class teacher came across the girl. She told, "Stand up! Don't be sad. You are going with us. Your parents have allowed you to go to a school trip." The girl became very happy.

THE MAGIC SHOW PART II

Around 9 O' clock in the morning the school bus left for the school trip. All the students sat in the bus with their respective class teacher. After twenty minutes they reached the venue. All students were in a queue.The students were sitting in a discipline. Soon the magician came. The magic started. There was a girl standing left on a stage. The magician told her to sleep in the box. Magician kept the plates on her body. The plates were so sharp that a girl can die but when they parted. The box with her body parts was so horrible. After few minutes the magician put of the plates from the box. And girl came safely from the box. The girl smiled and went back stage. The magician showed the other tricks. The magic is in his hat or from the hat. 'I really don't know. I saw the rabbit. Pigeon are coming from the hat. At first, the hat was empty. Suddenly a rabbit came after that a bird came. The magic was so unreal. All the students were shocked and confused. The same thing happened with the teachers also. They were also very surprised. There were many magic tricks. A small ten minutes interval happened. Students ate their snacks. Again MAGICIAN KARAN came on the stage. One after the other he showed magic tricks. We enjoyed a lot. At last show was over. All the students were back to school. The girl was very happy. THE MAGIC SHOW became memorable day for her.

I think magic is related to happiness. So it is not there all the time, but there are beautiful moments of magic in everyone's life.

Name : Gaurav Deepak Showkani, Class : III,

Year : 2019-2020

VARUN AND DHARA

Once upon a time there lived brother and sister named Varun and Dhara. Their parents were dead when they were small so they lived with their aunt and uncle. Their aunt was not kind at all. She even didn't love them. One day aunt thought of a plan she went to her husband and told we should leave the children in the center of the forest uncle was sad but did not want to break her heart, so he agreed.

Dhara was listening the plan she was shocked she knew that aunt and uncle do not love them she collected some stones the next day they started their journey. When they reached, their uncle told them to collect some sticks and started burning the fire, uncle entertain them with some stories when they slept uncle and aunt woke up and left the place.

When they woke up in the morning they saw their aunt and uncle were not there so they started crying Dhara told I have a plan I have thrown some stones on the ground we will follow the stones and reach back home they saw uncle standing on the gate, they ran and hugged him but aunt got very angry when she saw them the same night again aunt told to leave them uncle got sad but he agreed , Dhara now collected some seeds and threw them on the way uncle entertain them with some stories and they slept uncle and aunt left for the house.

The next morning they woke up Dhara told about the seeds when they were going back all the seeds were eaten by birds. They started crying and finding the way to the house, they saw chocolate house they felt hungry. Suddenly they heard beautiful voice of a lady; she was not an ordinary lady. She was a kind fairy she said what happened children.

Varun and Dhara told how there aunt and uncle cheated them the fairy felt bad and told them from now you can stay with me. Varun and Dhara agreed and they stay happily ever after.

Moral of the story

God has shared happiness among all his children. Just trust him.

Name: Nirvana Meena, Class: III, Year : 2019-2020

MIA AND THE LAND OF KIWIS

Mia and her younger brother Nick were very excited ,as like every year, this year also, their mom and dad have planned a trip abroad!This year the destination was New Zealand.

They were a family of four. Mia's dad was a business man. His name was Mark. He loved working out at gym. He was tall, handsome and looked younger for his age. Mia's mother use to work from home. She loved reading books, enjoyed cooking, dancing and was very fond of music. She was tall, fair, gorgeous and very kind. Her name was Stephanie.

Mia's brother Nick was 6 years old lanky boy. He was a super active and charming boy who loved playing cricket and irritating his elder sister. Mia on the other hand was a 9 years old girl who was intelligent, smart for her age and loved doing art and craft. She was thin, fair with long black hair where as Nick had curly hair with brown skin. But all four of them had one thing in common and that was their love for travelling!

Tickets were booked a month ago. The most exciting part about this trip was that it was going to be their first ever road trip abroad! Mia was finding it hard to contain her excitement. So she decided to do a little research of her own. She googled about New Zealand and found out that Kiwi is it's national bird and their longest river was called Waikato. Mom said that New Zealand is divided into twoislands - north and south.

They will be renting a car there and drive throughout the New Zealand. It's going to be a 15 days trip. Mia was finding it hard to sleep at night due to excitement. She kept dreaming about all the things she discovered on the google and what her parents have told her about their upcoming trip.

When their departure was just a day away, mom told Mia that she has booked a caravan stay for them for four nights! It means they were going to camp in New Zealand!

Wow! Mia thought - how exciting that would be to spend nights in caravan and do bonfire under the open sky!

The day had come for them to leave for their flight. Everything was packed. Mia was all dressed up for their long flight. She only wished her brother to be a little more obedient and a little less naughty as he was not listening to her and not getting ready. Mom had given her the responsibility to dress him up and see that all his things had been packed. Mia was used to taking care of her stuff from a very young age as her parent's love for travelling made sure that they were constantly travelling to new places every few months. But getting Nick and his things ready was very annoying. Anyways Mia decided to keep her cool and got Nick to get ready as they were leaving in about an hour.

After boarding the flight, Nick started with his usual mischiefs pulling Mia's hair, not letting her watch movies and snatching her art book to gain her attention. Only when mom scolded Nick, then only he stopped bothering Mia and after about two hours dozed off to sleep. Mia was now feeling peaceful and decided to watch her favourite cartoons. Mia heard air hostess making an announcement for landing to buckle up their seat belts as they were about to land. Mia had slept well and was feeling happy and fresh. Nick started shouting "we are in New Zealand". Mom quickly scolded him and asked him to keep quite.

There first city was Auckland. It took them quite long to collect luggage. Mia started feeling hungry. Mom and Nick had gone to the toilet. So Mia asked dad if she could get something to eat but dad told her that let's reach hotel first, then all of them can order something to eat.

They reached hotel quite late. When dad asked for room service, they told him that dinner time is over and they can only get sandwiches. Which made him angry but they had no choice. So they ordered a few sandwiches and went off to sleep.

Next day, they went for a city tour. Auckland was a beautiful city. They visited the famous sky tower. The view was magnificent from the top. Mia told mom how much fun it had been today.

Their next stop was Rotorua. While dad was driving,

Mia asked mom, what is special about this place? Mom told her that Rotorua is famous for hot water geysers from which hot water comes out like a fountain. Then there were lots of natural hot water springs. Nick started making faces when dad said that they will be going in a mud pool!

Mia was already imagining herself jumping into nice warm water as she loved water and swimming.

Next day Mia's dream came true. When they were returning from their visit to hot water geysers, mom spotted a board which was pointing towards a path to a hot water stream. They all decided to go there. After driving for about 10 minutes and with forests on both sides, they saw a parked van. Dad parked the car beside the van and all of them got out. They walked through a narrow path inside the woods and reached a spot where a family was swimming in the river stream. Mia could see smoke rising from the water. They also decided to jump in and played till sunset. After such a fun filled and memorable day, all of them crashed into their beds, tired and happy.

It has been 4 days and the time had come to visit Mia's most awaited place- THE HOBBITON!

Mia had seen this place in a movie called Lord of The Rings. She could not wait to see the little dwarf houses for real. The little colourful houses with round doors were like being in a fairy tale for real.Mia felt like she was playing a character in a story.

Afterwards they drove along a sea side road. Mia had never seen such beautiful blue colours of water. After crossing a number of vineyards, where mom said grape wines are made, and seeing a huge rainbow in the sky they reached the capital city of New Zealand - Wellington.

They checked into a hotel there. They were all getting ready to sleep after a long drive. Nick was brushing his teeth, just when he spotted a big spider hanging from the ceiling. He shouted and ran out! Even dad was afraid of spiders so he also jumped on the bed. Everyone started shouting so mom called the hotel staff to come and remove the spider. As the door bell rang Nick ran to open the door and crashed into the hotel staff who fell on the floor. Mom came rushing out to see if they were hurt. Dad apologised to the staff. Later the spider was removed and they finally got to sleep.

It had been a week in North New Zealand and it was time to go to south New Zealand. They took a cruise ferry to the South Island. The cruise was sailing through bluest waters through green mountains on both the sides. Mia and Nick stayed on the deck through out the ride.

When they reached Picton, Dad hired a new car and they started their drive through mountains, valleys, rivers and waterfalls. Mia could not believe her eyes that nature can be so beautiful. There were trees laden with flowers like she has never seen before. Herd of sheep, cows and rein deers. She saw lama which looked like a huge sheep with long neck. Kiwi crossed them on roads many times.

It was time for their long awaited caravan stay in Mapua city. Mia could not wait to reach there. Through the whole drive, they were singing songs and playing dumb charades. By the time they reached caravan, the sun was about to set. Mia and Nick quickly jumped out of the car and started exploring the place which is going to be their home for next 4 days. The caravan site was set on a farm surrounded with trees all around. There was a cute little pond with ducks in it. A bath tub was set on the deck of the pond. There were two caravans on the site. One was for sleeping and one for dinning. Mia and Nick named the red one -ruby and blue one bluey.

As it was getting colder, dad decided to do bon fire. And thus started their camping in New Zealand! Mia and Nick could not be happier. All of them sat around the fire, told each other stories and drank hot cocoa with marshmallows.

Next morning, Mia and Nick woke up early. Mom had already filled the bathtub with hot water for them to enjoy.

After bath and breakfast, all of them were ready to explore their property. There were trees with huge lemons and orange on them. They helped the owner in feeding the hens and sheep on the farm. Later they went to the sea shore and had lunch.

Staying in caravan surrounded with trees and water was so much fun! They even used a compost toilet for the first time in life!

It was a very memorable experience for all of them.

After enjoying their stay in caravan they drove along mountains and rivers and were about to reach Mount Cook for star gazing when their car got stuck in mud. It was getting darker and nobody seems to be coming their way. Mom and dad were getting worried now. They tried and tried but nothing happened. Dad was just thinking of calling any road service when somebody knocked on the car window. A man with a painted face and feathers on his head was using sign language, asking dad what was wrong. All of them got afraid at first. Then mom said, she has read about these people. They are Maories- tribe of New Zealand and are very helpful. So dad got out, made some gestures with his hands. The

Maori man called his men and all of them pushed the car out of the mud. Dad thanks them by Bowing in front of them. They smiled and made a sign, offering them food. First dad refused but then agreed. Nick was hiding in mother's lap the whole time. Mom and dad told him not to be afraid. They all went with the Maori people and ate fruits. They had a bonfire and small kids were dancing around it. Women were singing some kind of songs. It turned out to be a great adventure for them. Once again dad, mom, Mia and Nick said thanks and goodbyes and drove to their last destination, Christchurch. Through out the way, Mia kept thinking about those Maori people, their clothes, feather caps and face paint. They were all so nice and friendly. She thought they were very lucky that they got to meet them.

It was their last day in New Zealand and nobody wanted to go back. It had been such a wonderful trip which was full of beautiful sites, adventures and fun filled moments. Mia was a little sad. She wanted to live one more day in caravans, meet Maoris one more time. Then mom told her that they must-go back to their home. They will plan another wonderful trip next year and see new places which they have not seen before.

Mia knew in her heart that this trip will always be special for her.....

Name : Myara Sharma, Class : III, Year : 2019-2020

THE BRAVE BUNNIES

Once in a forest, there was a burrow. A mother rabbit and a baby rabbit lived in it.The bunny had a friend who was also a small little bunny and lived nearly. One day the mother rabbit was telling the bunnies a story .Once upon a time there lived a ferocious creature behind the bridge named the Carrot Bunny who snatched carrots. He had very "DIRTY JAWS" and "DIRTY PAWS" with big long YELLOW TEETH! The small bunnies pretended that they were not afraid of the carrot bunny in the story but actually they were!!!.The next evening, they went to find the carrot bunny! FREAKY!

They met a big Owl &they asked him "have you seen a

carrot bunny? “He laughed and said, what is that? There is no such thing as a carrot bunny!” The bunnies hopped out of the way to the jungle and walked back home.They slept that night and the next morning they asked the other animals if they had seen a carrot bunny.They asked the squirrel, monkey , birds n others too but they all said no.”NO WE HAVEN’T SEEN A CARROT BUNNY! Now don't disturb us, we have lot of work to do! The bunnies went back homeand very sadly told his mother we didn’t find any carrot bunny the whole day!!The mother laughed at her innocent bunnies and told them that she had made up the story of Carrot Bunny just to make them scared so that they don’t go to the bridge at night. As soon as the bunnies came to know about this they exhaled a sign of relief & they all lived happily ever after.

Moral of the story

Never believe in false stories!!

Name : Samara Sharma, Class : III, Year : 2019-2020

THE FOUR SPARROWS

Once in a thick forest there lived four sparrows in an oak tree.One was called "Snapper" and he collected twigs for their nest. The second was "Tripper" and he went in search for food. The third was called Cherry & he guarded their nest. The fourth one was "Coco"but he was too little to do anything.One day while the sparrows were playing a cat named Tom went off to chase Snapper &Triper, .Cherry & Coco went immediately to save their friends. Soon after, Cherry said, "Let's split up! It will be easy to find our friends" .Coco agreed with a smile on his face & soon, he was near a

Lake where he met a Sage.The Sage was looking for a book of Mantras (also called Rigveda) . The sage was very kind, so Coco decided to help him.Coco said "I 'm very small, I can't help, but still I'll try ! After a while of looking for the book coco exclaimed, Hurray! I found it!" As a reward the Sage gifted Coco,a boon saying.... "You shall have powers to create nature & to go heaven"

The chick was very happy &he went back. He spotted the cat &his friends. He noticed tom had caught Cherry too. He was a bit angry with his powers. He made the grass longer, made the sun shine brighter & made a humungous wall to block Tom. Tom lost them because of grass. He was blocked. Victory! They were united again & lived happily ever after

Moral of the story

Don't think little ones can't do anything Think positive!

Name : Pranshu Patel, Class : III, Year : 2019-2020

THE LOVELY FRIEND

Once upon a time, there was a boy named Harsh. He was very fond of keeping a pet with him and wished he would have a puppy to play with. One day his father came home and gave him a box of gift. He opened the gift and found a cute puppy from it. He loved the gift very much.

Every day when he comes from school, the puppy runs towards him. One night a robber entered into his house. The puppy saw him. He started barking towards him and pulled the blanket of Harsh, who was sleeping in his room.

By the voice of barking puppy, all family members woke

up. Harsh's father caught the robber and his mother called the police. Police came and took robber to the police station. Every one was thanking the puppy because of who robbery was prevented.

Moral of the story

Dogs and humans are the best and honest friends. A little creature cam sometime be as helpful as a human being.

Name : Khushil Lalwani, Class : III, Year: 2019 - 2020

NO FEE FOR THIS CHORE

"Rohit, please give me a glass of water," said Rohit's father. "Dad, I'm doing my homework. Please ask Divya to get it for you,"RepliedRohit from the living room, while continuing to read his book"Alright, son, at least do come over here to collect your pocket money.On seeing him Dad started laughing. He knew that though Rohit never helped around the house, he was always ready to collect his pocket money. After collecting the money, Rohit went to his books. Later, Dad called out again, "Rohit, will you please give me today's newspaper?" "Dad, I'm studying. Please do not disturb me," replied Rohit.

"Rohit, I forgot to give you money to buy the books you had asked for. Please come over and collect it", said Dad. Rohit ran up to him. Dad knew that whatever money was left after buying the books. Rohit will add it to his piggy bank. Dad kept laughing as he gave money to Rohit. Although Rohit was puzzled by Dad's behavior, he did not ask him about it. As Rohit walked back to the living room, his father called him again. This time too, Rohit went running to him. He thought that his father was going to give him more pocket money. But his father started laughing.Rohit was annoyed. "Dad, why are you laughing?" he asked. "I am laughing at your greed, son," replied Dad. "I did not tell you why I called you, but you came back running thinking I was going to give you more money. You would not get up to help me, but you were willing to interrupt your studies to collect your pocket money."

Rohit felt ashamed of his behavior. He quietly walked away. He came back with a glass of water and the newspaper and quietly placed them on his father's desk. Dad then offered some money to Rohit, but he refused to take it. "I am sorry, Dad, I should have given you the water and newspaper when you had requested for them. I will not take money for this," said Rohit.Dad hugged him and said, "It's alright, son. Remember, never be greedy abut money and always respect your eleders," Rohit nodded and hugged his father back.

Moral of the story

We should always serve our parents. Parents take a lot of pain to nurture their children.

Name : Ahaan Bindlesh, Class : IV, Year: 2019- 2020

"GREED NEVER WINS - TALE OF TWO BROTHERS"

Once upon a time in a village in France near the coastal town of Nice, there lived two brothers born in a wealthy family. The smaller brother was James and the elder brother was John.

The younger brother James was a very intelligent but very shy guy. The elder John, on the other hand was not all intelligent and smart like his brother but he was a very loud boy. All the villagers however thought that

James was an addle boy who remains confused in his thoughts and John was wise boy who thinks and does things very clearly and nicely.

The parents of both the boys had tragically died in an accident after a few years they were born. They had left behind lot of wealth for their children to live comfortably.

The pet name of John was "brain of a fox" and the pet name of James was "brain of a donkey".

John had many friends but James had none because of their nature. All the villagers wanted to remain close to John but used to shy away from James.

As mentioned they had a large house and had huge property with them. But before dying their father gave 75% of the property to his elder son John whom he always thought was more mature and the remainder 25% to younger James. Both the brothers stayed in the same house and looked after the family business

But one day John threw out James from their house. James protested saying "this is my part which my fatherhad left for me."

But John who had the bigger share said "But you are not good and I am more intelligent than you are and then I am the one who is running the full business. You are being just a burden to us".

James replied that "I am more intelligent". John upon hearing this laughed and closed the door.

James left the house with a heavy heart but he did not cry.

James worked day and night and finally he was able to

make a small house for himself and with hard work, he was living comfortably.

Where as John who took away the entire business was in a huge debt. The business had given him huge losses as he could not run his company well.

There was a buzz in the village that some big man from the city of Paris named Thomas was going to buy John's company in the auction.

People from nearby villages flocked to see the auction and also to see who the gentleman from Paris has come to buy John's business. James though reluctant to go at first thought of going to the auction and see for himself. John entire business was taken away by Thomas in the auction.

He requested crying to Thomas to give him one more chance to come out of loss and save his business.Soafter thinking Thomas said to John "if you will give correct answers to my questions, I will give your company back".

To which the first question Thomas asked was...... "What is that comes 2 (twice) times in a week, 1 (Once) time in a year and none in a month".

And the second question was, "What is the thing that the more we take, the more we keep leaving behind.

John came in big trouble as he was not able to get the answer. He thought, thought and thought and as hard as he could, but he could not come up with the reply.

He requested the villagers to help him with the answer but none of them could help him give the answer.

James who was watching the whole thing from a distance came forward to help out his brother. He knew the answers of

Thomas questions.

He said the answer to the first question is "E"

And the answer to his second question is "Footsteps".

Thomas was very impressed with James answers and said "James you are a very intelligent guy and I am very happy with your answers".

And he then said "I am ready to give John a second chance and give him back his business as promised".

John realised his mistake he made with James by throwing him out of the house. He said sorry to James and asked for his forgiveness.

James was a happy man as John decided to give him more from his share and welcomed him back to the house.

James and John lived happily thereafter.

Moral of the story

The story teaches us that greed never makes you win and we must learn to remain humble in life and we should respect relations.

Name : Ryan Bunsal, Class : IV, Year : 2019-20

LITTLE BRO, BIG SIS

Once upon a time there were two children Aditya and Aditi. Aditi was 10 years old and elder sister of Aditya who was 5 years. One day it was Sunday and it was Aditya's birthday, his parents, sister and he himself was at home. When all of the family members got up, He said it is my birthday so I want to be king for one day. Everyone agreed. First he ordered his sister to takeout his clothes from the cupboard .And then he said to his mother that I want to eat items made up of chocolate in breakfast. Then he said his father to bring new toys for him to play. After bathing and eating his breakfast he went to sleep. When he woke up he saw there was no one in the house. He searched for them but he couldn't find them. He thought for a while that as I was ordering everyone from morning I think that they have left the house. Then he thought that they must be in garden. He went in the garden in search of his parents he didn't find them in the garden. When he was going inside the house he saw balloons in his father's car. He opened the car and saw his family. He said sorry to his family and said I will never repeat this mistake again.

Moral of the Story

We should not be selfish.

Name : Sharanya Bindlish, Class : IV, Year : 2019-2020

Celebrate With Poems

A Collection of Acrostic Poems on 'Festivals of India'

DIWALI

D Diya's, rangoli and toran
I Igniting the sprit and soul
W wishes for good health and happiness
A All nights' shine and sparkle
L lights and candles all around

I ignore sadness and invite friends and family

HOLI

H Happy colorful festival

O opportunity to clear misunderstandings & remove bitterness in relations

L live in peace and harmony with every one

I indulging and saying "Bura Na Mano HoliHai

EID

E Enjoy with every one and have "sevaiya"

I Islam is great

D doing the best while fasting

RAMADAN

R Read Quran everyday

A Assist table sitting for Iftar

M Make sure to be kind to your friends and family

A Avoid being angry

D Distribute charity

A All-night Amaal

N Now ready for "EID"

GURPURAB

G Guru nanakji

U Understands all our problems

R Respect for everyone

P Praying for peace

U Ushers us on the right path

R Right guidance

A Acknowledge the good in others

B Baba ji always bless us to be a good human being

CHRISTMAS

C Christ was born today

H Holy night

R Requesting Santa for gifts

I I am waiting

S Singing carols

M Making cakes and cookies

A Angels will bless us

S Santa Claus is coming

Name: Manan Bhambhani, Class: IV, Year: 2019-20

THE NATURAL HAIKU

[ACROSTIC POEMS]

FOREST

FROM THE BIGGEST TO THE SMALLEST
OR THE SHORTEST TO THE TALLEST
RATS LIKE FEST OR COCKROACHES LIKE PEST
EVERYTHING LIVES IN THE FOREST.
SO WE SHOULD NOT BREAK THIS BEAUTIFUL CHEST

TO SAVE THE BIGGEST, TALLEST AND SMALLEST.....

RAIN

ROW OF CLOUDS IN THE SKY

ASTOUNDINGLY SHOWERING WATER TILL THEY FLY

IN THAT WATER BLESSINGS LIE

NATURE IN THE FORM OF RAIN GIVES THE FEELING OF HEAVEN, JUST TRY

SUN

SUN THE MAIN SOURCE OF ENERGY

UNBELIEVABLE! THE SUN AND THE EARTH GIVE SHINE

TO THE WORLD WITH THEIR SYNERGY

NEVER UNDERESTIMATE THE POWER OF THE SUN AS NO

ENERGY MEANS FULL LETHARGY

PLANETS

PLANETS ARE HERE PLANETS ARE THERE

LIKE A VERY BIG SPHERE

ALL OF THEM MOVED UP AND DOWN

NOW THEY ALL MOVE ROUND AND ROUND

ENTERING THE WORLD OF PLANETS? TAKE

INTEREST AND DON'T STRESS

TALK TO THEM AND ALWAYS HELP THEM THE BEST

SO TODAY WE LEARNT A LESSON ON PLANETS OUR BEST FRIENDS.

Name : Anvesha Agarwal Name : Ameena Khatri
Class : III, Year : 2019-2020

Poems for a week

1. <u>My cutest panda</u>

   My panda, my cutest little panda sleeping under a tree,
   Dreaming to eat bamboo leaves free.

2. <u>My fast pencil</u>

   My fast pencil, Oh my pencil, write fast and fast
   Help me to score good marks.

3. <u>The lost Key</u>

   I lock my house with a key I saw a monkey on a tree,
   I took the key to the sea but I lost the key at three

Luckily the monkey helped me

But a bee bite me and I got service for free

But I was not feeling good, that's why I didn't went back for my tea.

4. <u>My bright Sun</u>

My sun, my big, big bright sun,

Comes from the east and goes to the west,

Bye, bye little sun come again and again

5. <u>The Fairy Poem</u>

Oh how are you? Beautiful fairy

You are a pearl for me, my friends and everyone.

The colors of the rainbow that bound you,

The mesmerizing colours of your land

The beautiful creatures help you stand.

6. <u>The little thief</u>

I want the sweetest bun, but it guided by a famous nun,

I want to shoot it buy a gun but I will be punish in the sun,

I have no way except take it and run.

7. <u>My Treat</u>

I got a treat, I sat to eat,

I called my friends but they gave me good beat,

I met him in a street, he was sitting on a seat with the packet of wheat,

I ran away because there was too much heat.

Name : Vedanth Achanta, Class : IV Yamuna

Year : 2019-2020

Kites

Up in the air
See the kites fly,
Like coloured birds
In the wind-whipped sky.
I wish I was small
And as light as air,
I would climb on a kite

And sail up there.
Then I'd drift upon
The paper wings,
And hear the song
That the breezy wind sings.
Then I would sail high
Highest in the town,
So high in the sky
That I'd be the city's crown.
At the end of the day
I'd enjoy the moonlight,
I would not want to land
But it was night.
When it was time to sleep
I would land my fly flight.
And never be able to forget
This spectacular sight.

Name : Akshi Sharma, Class : IV, Year : 2019-2020

This is a story of a proud daughter Kaya

Kaya had a beautiful family mother father and younger brother. Her father was an army officer. She was living in a Delhi with family. Kaya used to miss father a lot whenever her father call she used to Bloom like a flower. All the time she pray to God "I want to see my father."

God heard her prayers. Father called his family to visit glacier. Kaya was very excited, the day came when they landed to a place called Thoise.She was amazed to see the beauty of the land. Snow clapped peaks with blue sky. But among all these scenic beauty Kaya's eyes were searching for someone. All men were looking same in uniform. She was confused but there one man was coming to them with big smile and open arms. Ahh!! It was Kaya's father.

Kaya jumped high and hugged him very tightly. Kaya's father took them to his camp. Kaya's father told her many stories of brave soldiers who have sacrificed their life for nation

Slowly time passed. Now it was time to say goodbye, they have lovely time for a month. Kaya was feeling upset but father promise her that he will visit them soon.

While coming back they faced a landslide. Big big rocks falling down lots of people were getting hurt. Kaya's father saw it. He made his family stand in the corner and run to help others. Kaya felt very bad ,we are his family how he can leave us. He should think of us first.

But there her father and other soldiers were running to save people. And finally when he rescued other people he came back for his family. He wrapped Kaya and we younger brother in a blanket and rushed towards other end. Mamma also ran behind us.

Once they reached, Kaya asked her father why did you left us for other people? Father replied with a smile " My dear you are my family but being a soldier , my first duty is to protect nation and its people. First I belong to my country then to you"

Before Kaya could understand people start clapping and thanking her father for saving their life.

Now Kaya got all her answers and she was feeling proud to be a daughter of a soldier.

Name : Devashya Thapliyal, Class : IV, Year : 2019-2020

TEACHINGS OF MAHAGURU AND GURU

I am DevashyaThapliyal. I am going to share my life experience here as I feel we learn a lot from our own experience.

One day my father asked me what I wanted to become in future.

I replied, "A cricketer!" Because I love to play.

My father said, "Ok, I will take you to your cricket coach or we can say your cricket Guru"

But I informed my father that the mother had told me that you are my Guru.

Father smiled and said – Yes, my child.She is right but for right path and right destination we all chose a guru, who takes us to our aim."

I nodded my head – Oh! But father if you are not my guru ...then (I think) yes...you are my MAHAGURU. Father smiled and hugged me.

Next day my MAHAGURU took me to my cricket GURU. He is our JADEJA Sir He is a very calm and lovely person. More importantly he taught me with passion and love.He once took me to the Indian Star Cricketer 'RAVINDRA JADEJA'. My GURU understood my feelings as well.

One day he told me that his leg has been injured and so he was going for a surgery and would be back after two months. I was sad. I didn't even like to go to the ground. My MAHAGURU was worried. One day he asked me – Devashya, why are you not going to the ground? He said – Cricket and the ground is your aim of your life.If you want another coach I can arrange for you.I told my MAHAGURU – No, I don't want any other. If my GURU do not come for two months, I will also not go to the ground.

My MAHAGURU hugged me and told me –Oh my Dear! You respect your teacher and you can feel yourteacher's pain as well .You and your GURU have a beautiful bond .God bless you! Now you are in right path!

After two months when my GURU came back, I joined

him happily. I thanked God.

MORAL OF THE STORY:

Respect and love your parents and teachers. They give you your right path!

Name : Saish, Class : IV, Year : 2019-20

PARENTS

I am Saish and I am 9 years old. I have a lovely family of 4 people who are my mom, my dad,my cute little sister and me. Friends, today I want to tell you a story which is my real life incident!

I love cricket and I play it everyday but my mom *shouts* that don't play outdoor games inside the house. But I didn't listen to her because we enjoy playing cricket.

One day Dad came home and I shouted "Hurray" and I slipped while playing cricket and I fell on my face because of that my front tooth broke and I started crying!When my mom saw me she also started crying.After that I realized my mistake and I felt very bad so I hugged my mom and said sorry.

Moral

So friends moral of the story is always listen to your parents because it is for your own good.

www.ingramcontent.com/pod-product-compliance
Ingram Content Group UK Ltd.
Pitfield, Milton Keynes, MK11 3LW, UK
UKHW020634170826
14477UKWH00055B/367